WALT DISNEY PRODUCTIONS
presents

Scamp Learns a Lesson

Random House New York

First American Edition. Copyright © 1982 by The Walt Disney Company. All rights reserved under International and Pan-American Copyright Conventions. Published in the United States by Random House, Inc., New York, and simultaneously in Canada by Random House of Canada Limited, Toronto. Originally published in Denmark as VAKS STIKKER AF by Gutenberghus Gruppen, Copenhagen. ISBN: 0-394-85516-7 Manufactured in the United States of America

3 4 5 6 7 8 9 10   D E F G H I J K L

One evening Lady and the Tramp and their puppies were lying in front of the fire.

Their people, Darling and Jim, were sitting nearby on the sofa.

Everything was quiet and peaceful.

But with a puppy named Scamp in the house, things would not be quiet for long!

Jim stood up and stretched.

"I need some air," he said. "Who wants to take a walk?"

Only Lady wanted to go. She ran and got her leash.

"See you in a little while," said Jim.
"Tramp, you take care of the house."
Lady tugged at her leash and led Jim
outdoors.

The puppies gathered
around Tramp.

"Tell us a story,"
they begged.

"Tell us about the
good old days!" said
Scamp.

"Ah, the good old
days!" said Tramp.
"That was before
I settled down
with your mother
to raise a family."

"I used to run around town with my good friends, Trusty and Jock," said Tramp. "We went where we pleased."

"We always ate at
the best restaurants—
the ones with back-door
service. What feasts
we had!"

"The dogcatcher used to chase us, but we could outsmart him any day. Only careless dogs got caught and taken to the dog pound."

"On sunny days we went to the zoo
and said hello to the animals there.
Sometimes a man gave us ice cream."

"We ended every evening in
the park, singing to the moon.
Ah, that was the life!"

Tramp talked until
Lady came back with
Jim.

"Oh, Tramp!" said
Lady. "You've been
telling your stories
again. You'll give
the children ideas!"

"It's time for bed, children," said Lady. "Come along now."

Soon everyone was asleep—everyone except
Scamp.

He kept thinking about Tramp's stories.

He wished he could run around town too.

The next morning Aunt Sara came to take the puppies for a walk in the park.

Scamp was not happy to see Aunt Sara. Walking with Aunt Sara was always so boring.

"Good morning, Scamp!" said Aunt Sara.
"And how are we today?"
"Ugh!" thought Scamp.

"Now hold still!" said Aunt Sara.
She put a leash on Scamp's collar.
Scamp scowled.

Off went Aunt Sara with the puppies.

The puppies had to stay on the leash.

They had to do what Aunt Sara said.

"Phooey!" thought Scamp. "I want to run around town like Tramp!"

Aunt Sara sat down on a park bench.
After a while she dozed off.
"Here's my chance!" thought Scamp,
and he tiptoed away.

Then he raced
out of the park!

Scamp ran through street after street.
He felt so happy and bold that he ran
right in front of the dogcatcher.
"Only careless dogs get caught!"
said Scamp, and he raced off.

Suddenly Scamp was jerked to a stop.

His leash had caught on a fireplug.

Scamp pulled and pulled on the leash.
He pulled so hard that...

his collar popped off!

Some wonderful new
smells reached Scamp.
"It must be the zoo!"
he said.

He trotted across
the street.

No dogs were allowed in the zoo,
but Scamp didn't know that.

He walked right in.

The gatekeeper was busy and
didn't see him.

Scamp barked hello to the lion family.

The lions roared back.

Scamp barked hello to the monkeys.

The monkeys chattered and laughed.

What fun the zoo was!
No one gave Scamp
any ice cream.
But the elephant
gave him a bath!

"My, the animals are noisy today!"
said the gatekeeper.

Then he spotted Scamp.

"How did that dog get in here?"
he wondered.

"Here, doggie! Nice doggie!" said
the gatekeeper.

Scamp ran happily to the man.

The gatekeeper called over a policeman.

"This little dog is lost," the gatekeeper said. "And he has no collar."

"Then he belongs in the dog pound," said the policeman. "Give him to me."

And before Scamp knew it, he was locked in the dogcatcher's cart.

Off he went to the pound!

Back home Aunt Sara was saying,
"I looked all over the park for Scamp.
But I couldn't find him anywhere."
"Oh, dear," said Darling. "He's such
a little dog. I hope he's all right."
Everyone was very worried.

"Where could that
rascal be?" said Tramp.
"You should know,"
said Lady. "You told
him all those stories!"

"Scamp could be anywhere," said Tramp.
"I guess I'd better look for him."

Tramp sat up and
barked loudly at Jim.
"You want to find
Scamp, don't you,"
said Jim. "Let's go!"

Tramp led the way,
sniffing Scamp's trail.

Sniff...sniff...sniff...
Tramp followed his nose.

Tramp found Scamp's collar and leash.

"Good boy!" said Jim. "You're on the right track!"

Scamp's trail led right to the zoo.

Tramp was not surprised.

The zoo was about to close.
"Wait! Please!" called Jim.
"Have you seen a little lost dog?"

"Why, yes," said the gatekeeper.
"I found a cute little scamp
with no collar. He's down at
the dog pound now."

"Thanks!" said Jim,
and he hailed a taxi.

Jim and Tramp rode to the dog pound.
Would they ever see Scamp again?
The little puppy had no collar.
Nobody knew his name and address.
Anyone who wanted a pet could
take him home.

"A brown puppy with no collar?" said
the clerk at the dog pound. "I'll have
to check the book. We have a lot of dogs
in the pound today."

But Tramp knew
Scamp was there.
He could hear
the puppy barking.

The clerk opened the door to the dog pens,
and Tramp ran right to his son.

He was so happy to see Scamp!

And Scamp was very happy to see his father.

Jim paid a fine to free Scamp.

Then he took the dogs home in a taxi.

"Look who we found!" called Jim.

Lady was not surprised when she heard what had happened.

"Oh, those stories of yours!" she said to Tramp.

Lady gave Scamp a scolding.

Jim gave Scamp a scolding too.
"No more running off," he said.
"You were very lucky this time."

And he put Scamp's
collar back on.

"I hope you've learned your lesson,"
said Tramp. "Running around town is not
for little dogs."

"I'm sorry," said Scamp in a small voice.
But he couldn't wait till he got big!